I Wish
I Liked
Green Peas

By Sarah Keane
Illustrated by Mitch Vane

HOUGHTON MIFFLIN COMPANY
BOSTON
ATLANTA   DALLAS   GENEVA, ILLINOIS   PALO ALTO   PRINCETON

I wish I liked green peas,

green beans, broccoli, and spinach.

But I *don't*!

What I *do* like are chocolate-chip cookies.

I wish I liked tidying up,

staying inside, sitting still, and going to bed early.

But I *don't*!

What I *do* like is playing outside until dark.

I wish I liked pink dresses,

my hair in ribbons, lacy socks, and shiny shoes.

11

But I *don't*!

What I *do* like are my old jeans.

I wish I liked
going to the dentist,
sloppy kisses,
piano practice, and
fighting with my brother.

BUT I DON'T!

But I *do* like Carla,
my best friend.

And she likes
green peas *and*
green beans *and*
spinach *and*
tidying up *and*
pink dresses!